SPIEGELMAN, NADJA
ZIG AND WIKKI IN THE COW : A
BOOK /
2015.
37565007601171   GUER

P9-DFS-948

SONOMA COUNTY
LIBRARY
OFFICIAL
DISCARD

ZIG AND WIKKI

in

THE COW

NADJA SPIEGELMAN & TRADE LOEFFLER

ZIG AND WIKKI in THE COW

Hey! Come look at this little guy!
Pay attention to ME, Zig!

A TOON BOOK BY

NADJA SPIEGELMAN & TRADE LOEFFLER

TOON BOOKS IS AN IMPRINT OF CANDLEWICK PRESS

ABDO Spotlight

For Dash *–Nadja*
For Annalisa, Clark, and Boo *–Trade*

Editorial Director: FRANÇOISE MOULY
Book Design: FRANÇOISE MOULY & JONATHAN BENNETT
Guest Editor: GEOFFREY HAYES
Wikki's Screen Drawings: MYKEN BOMBERGER
TRADE LOEFFLER'S artwork was drawn in black ink on paper and colored digitally

ABDOPUBLISHING.COM

Reinforced library bound edition published in 2015 by Spotlight, a division of ABDO
PO Box 398166, Minneapolis, Minnesota 55439. Spotlight produces high-quality reinforced library bound
editions for schools and libraries. Published by agreement with Candlewick Press.

Printed in the United States of America, North Mankato, Minnesota.
112014
012015

THIS BOOK CONTAINS
RECYCLED MATERIALS

A TOON Book™ © 2012 RAW Junior, LLC, 27 Greene Street, New York, NY 10013. TOON Books® is an
imprint of Candlewick Press, 99 Dover Street, Somerville, MA 02144. No part of this book may be used or
reproduced in any manner whatsoever without written permission except in the case of brief quotations
embodied in critical articles and reviews. All photos used by permission. Page 8: © Igor Burchenkov /
iStockphoto.com; Page 16: © 2011 Kyle Slade; Page 19: © Zralok / Dreamstime.com; Page 20: © Shariffc
/ Dreamstime.com; Page 21: © Vlue / Dreamstime.com; Page 33: Slides © Mel Yokoyama; Page 40: Cow
mouth © 2011 Keven Law (http://www.flickr.com/photos/kevenlaw/), Cow tongue © Kurt / Dreamstime.com,
Cow nose © 2011 Jessica Warren; Back cover: Cow © Tilo / Dreamstime.com. TOON Books®, LITTLE LIT®
and TOON Into Reading™ are trademarks of RAW Junior, LLC. All rights reserved.

LIBRARY OF CONGRESS CATALOGING-IN-PUBLICATION DATA

This book was previously cataloged with the following information:

Spiegelman, Nadja.
Zig and Wikki in The cow : a TOON book / by Nadja Spiegelman & [illustrated by] Trade Loeffler.
p. cm.
Summary: Two extraterrestrial friends land on Earth in the center of a farm ecosystem, where an argument
forces them to separate, only to be brought back together in the stomach of a cow.
ISBN 978-1-935179-15-3 (hardcover)
1. Graphic novels. [1. Graphic novels. 2. Extraterrestrial beings--Fiction. 3. Farms--Fiction. 4. Flies--Fiction.]
I. Loeffler, Trade, ill. II. Title. III. Title: Cow.
PZ7.7.S65Zj 2012   741.5'973--dc23   2011026676

ISBN 978-1-61479-306-9 (reinforced library bound edition)

Spotlight

A Division of ABDO
abdopublishing.com

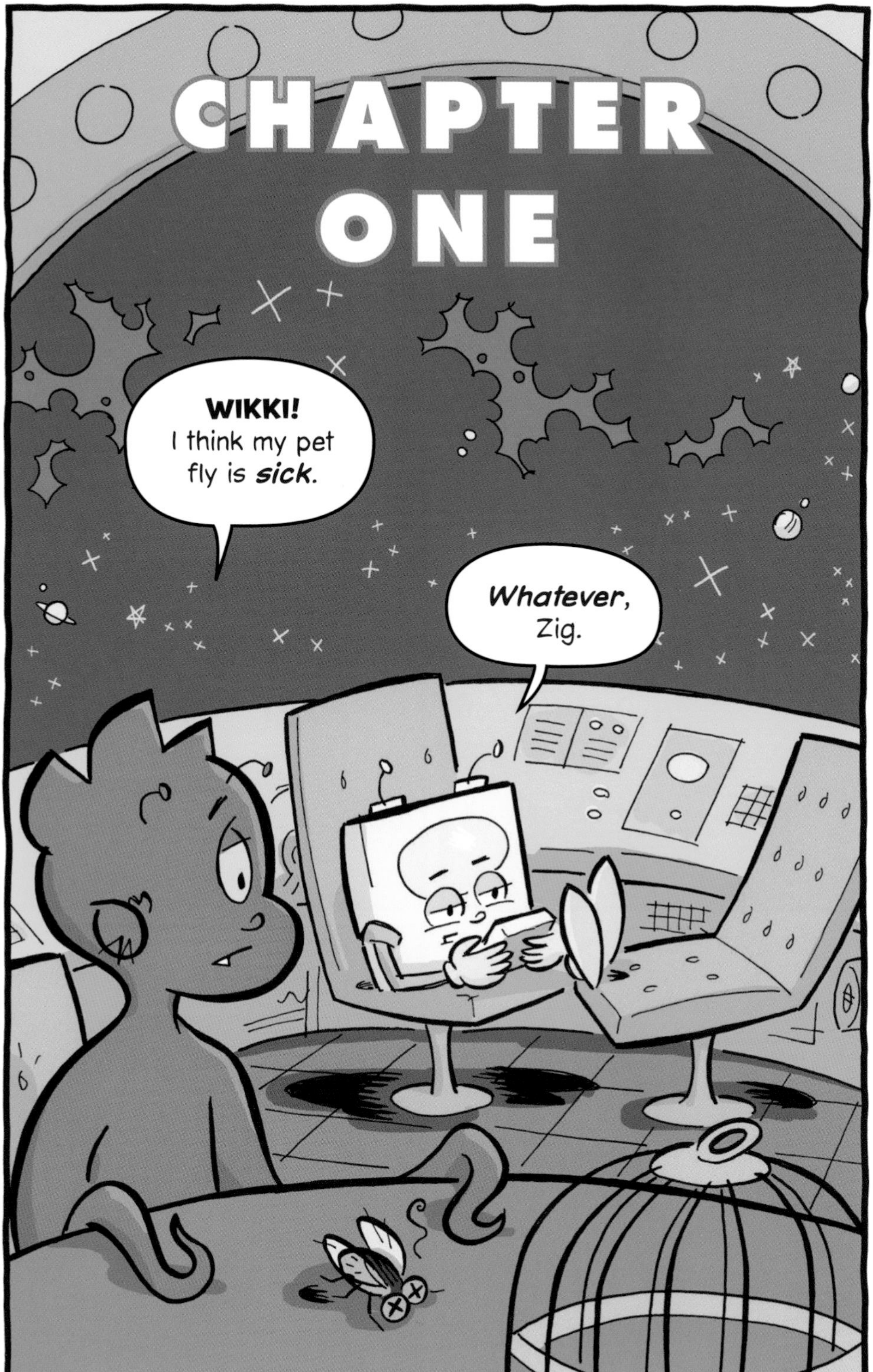
CHAPTER ONE
WIKKI! I think my pet fly is *sick*.
Whatever, Zig.

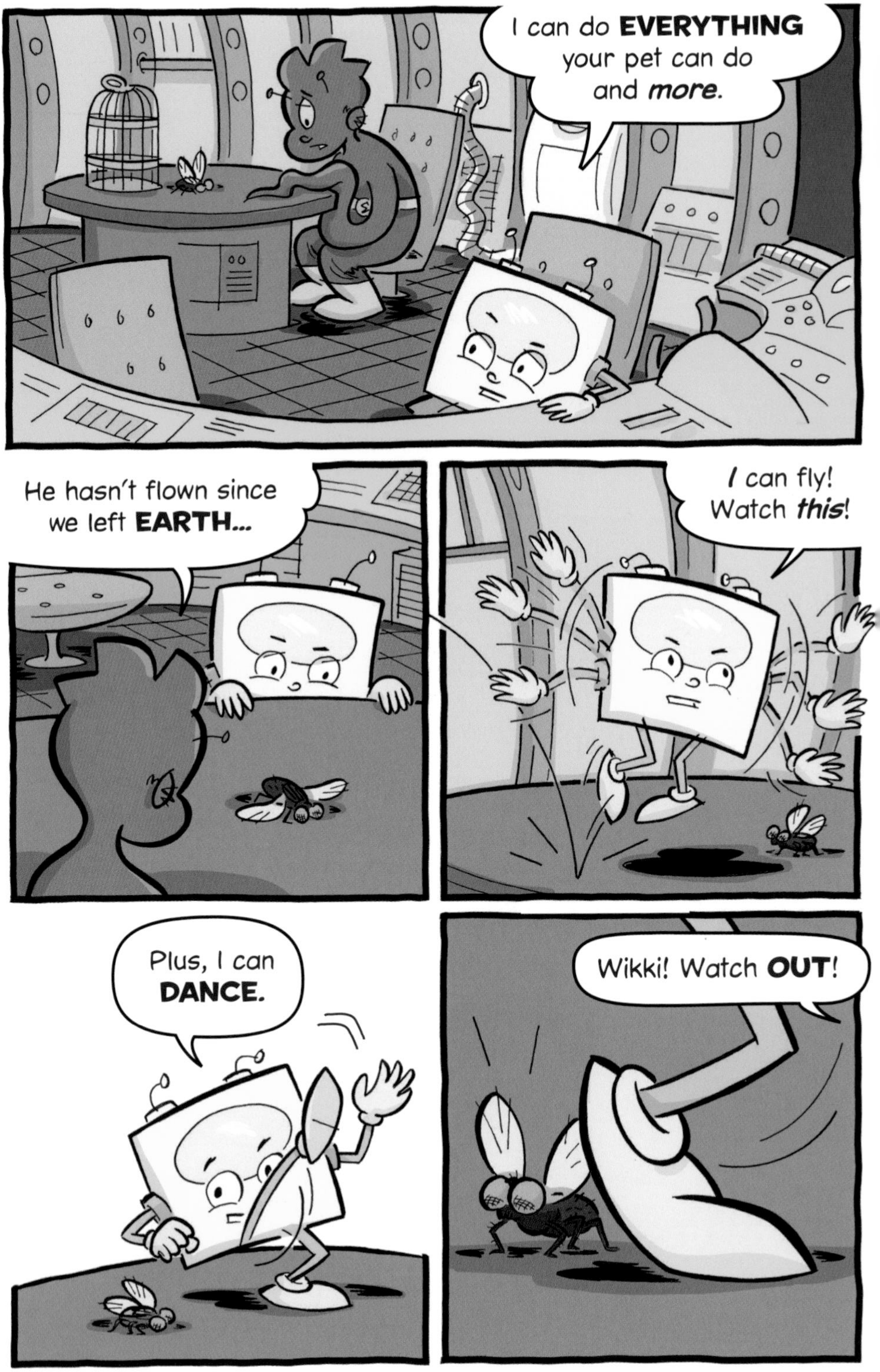
I can do **EVERYTHING** your pet can do and ***more***.
He hasn't flown since we left **EARTH...**
I can fly! Watch ***this***!
Plus, I can **DANCE.**
Wikki! Watch **OUT**!

7

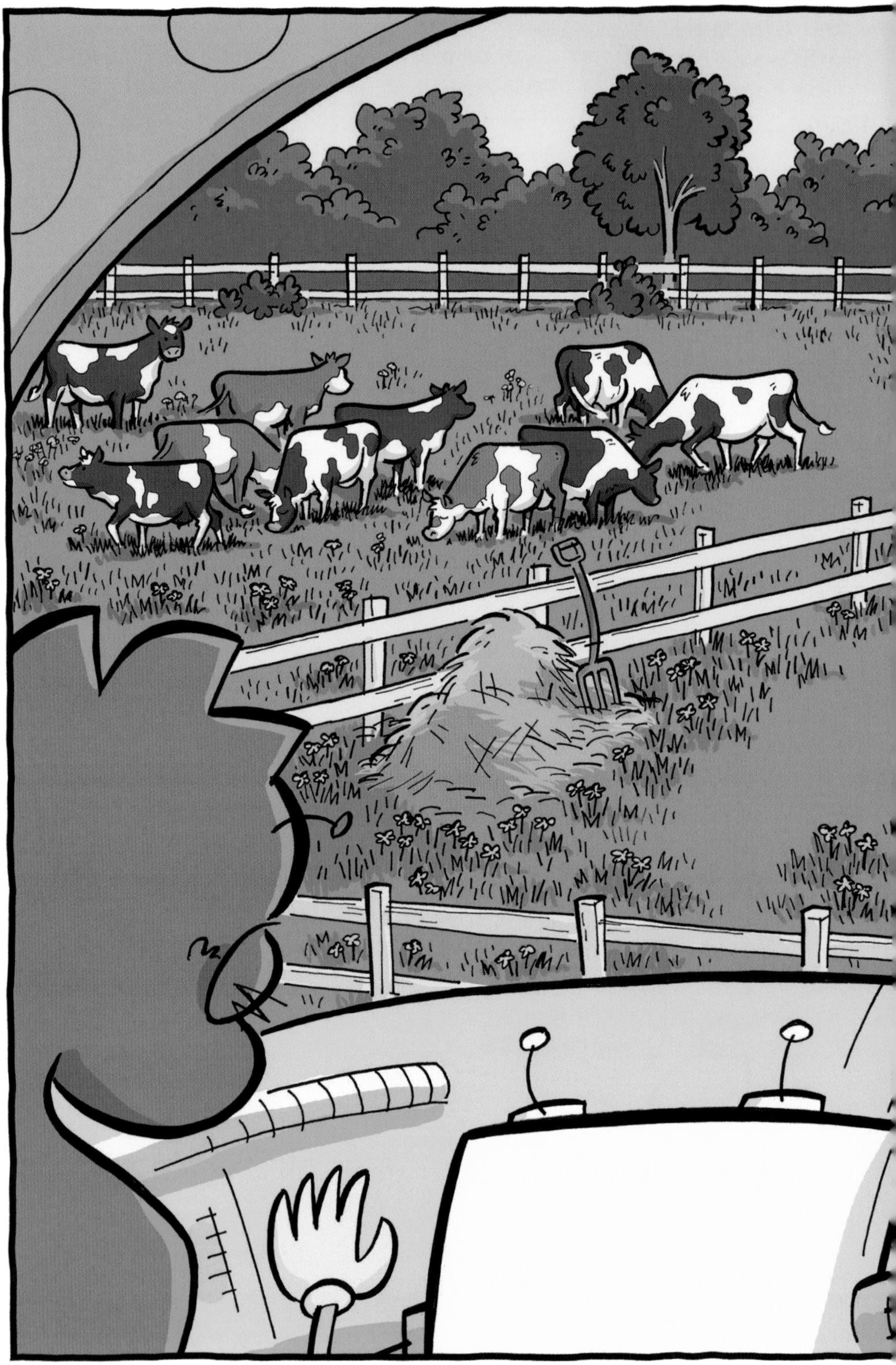

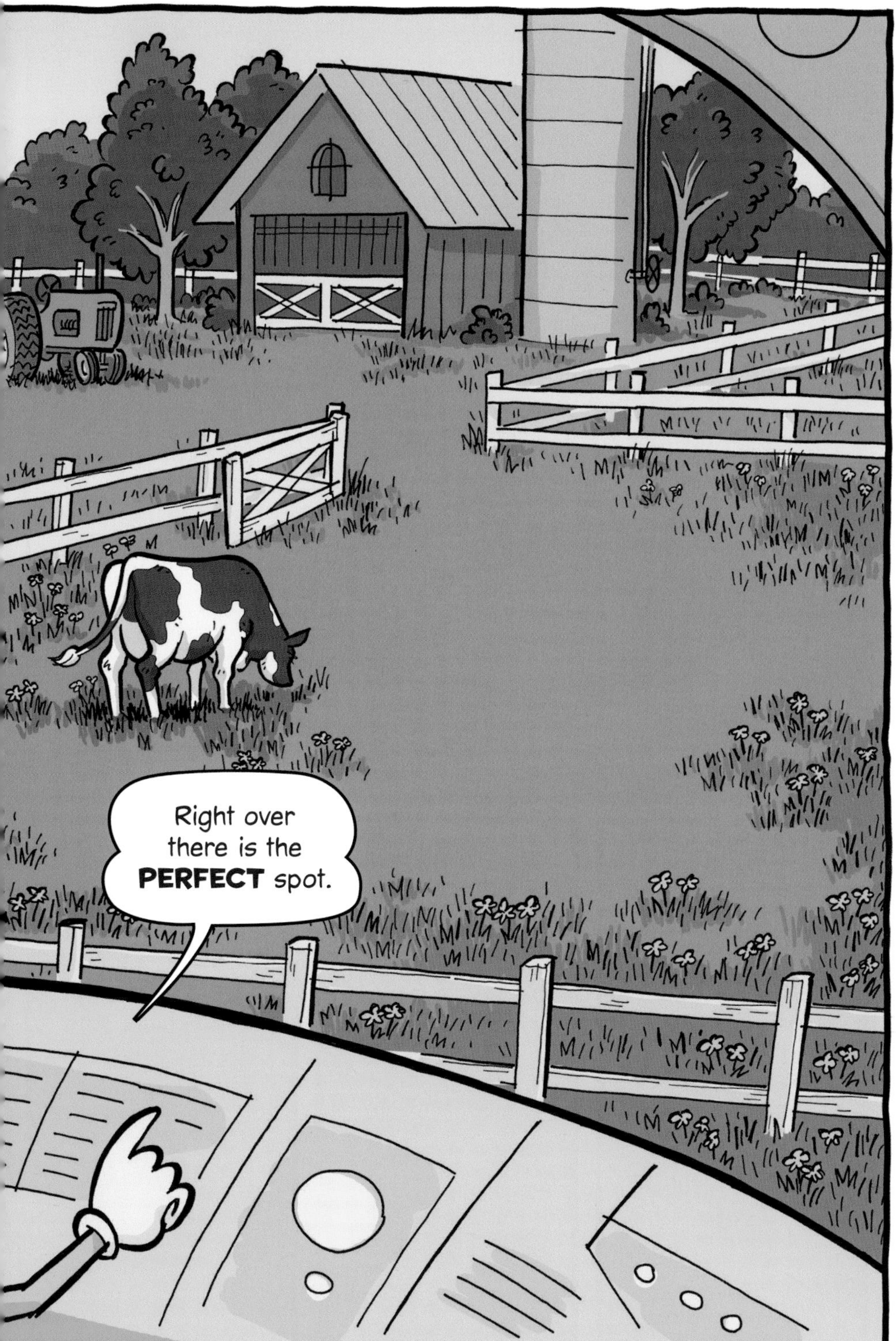
Right over there is the **PERFECT** spot.

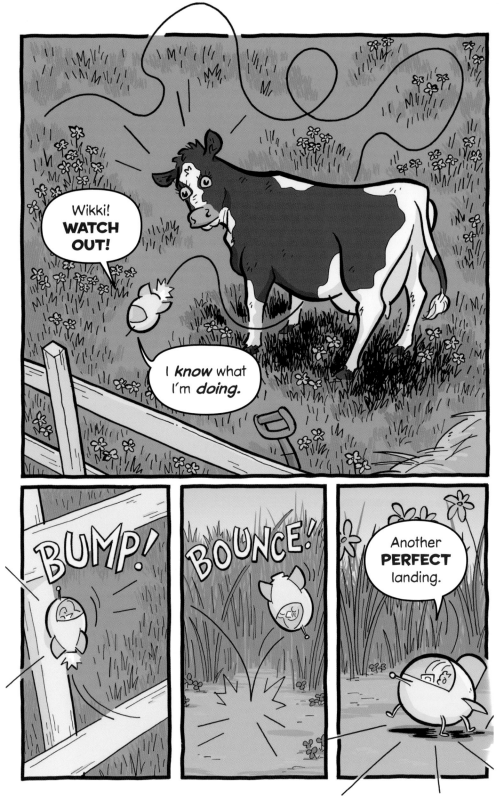

13

RUMINANTS

ANIMALS WHO HAVE SPECIAL STOMACHS, LIKE COWS, GOATS AND DEER, CAN GET ENERGY FROM EATING GRASS.

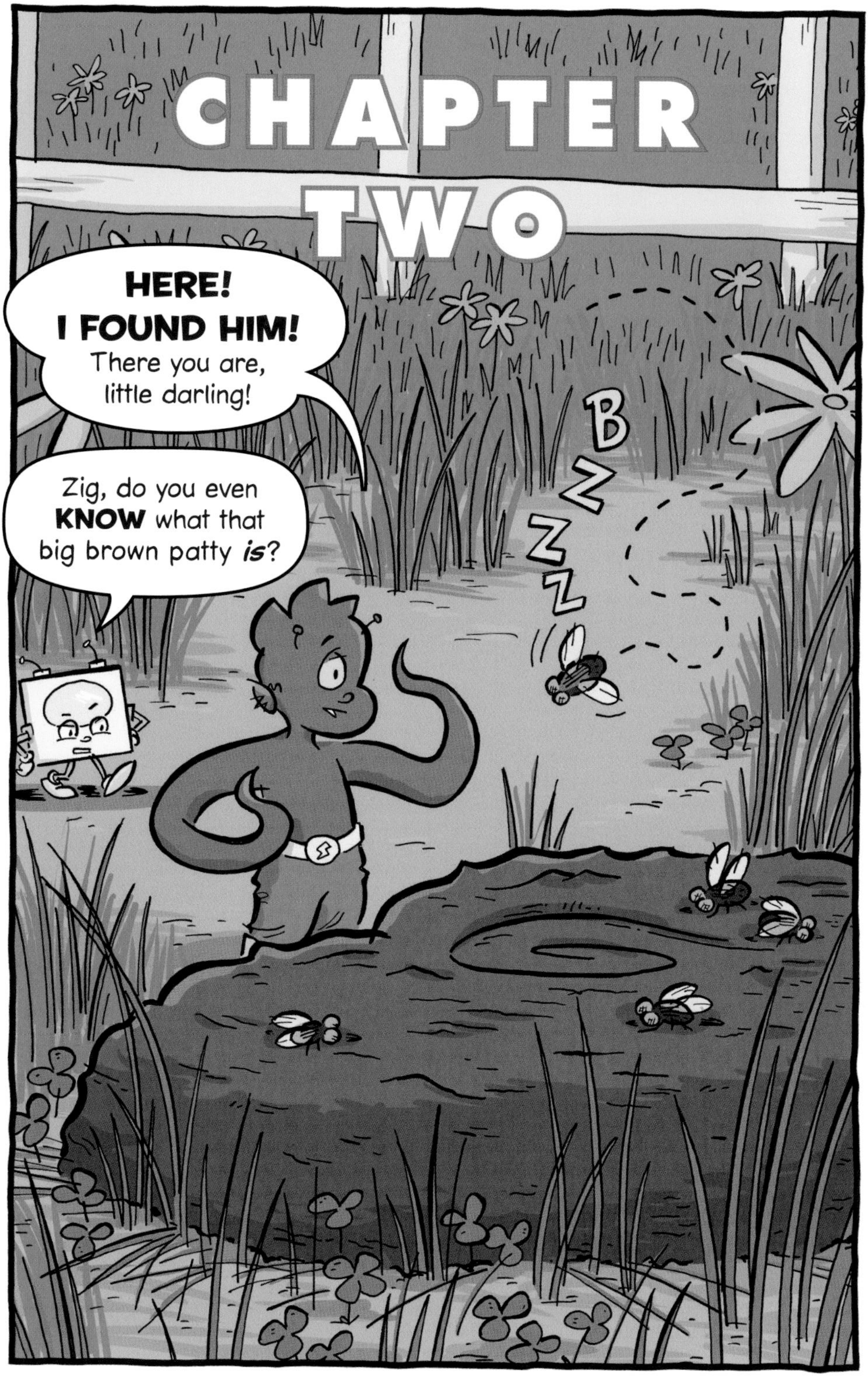
CHAPTER TWO
HERE! I FOUND HIM! There you are, little darling!
Zig, do you even **KNOW** what that big brown patty *is*?
BZZZ

17

DUNG BEETLES

THERE ARE THREE TYPES OF DUNG BEETLES: *ROLLERS* ROLL BALLS OF DUNG AWAY TO BURY UNDERGROUND, *DWELLERS* LIVE IN THE DUNG, AND *TUNNELERS* BUILD TUNNELS IN THE SOIL.

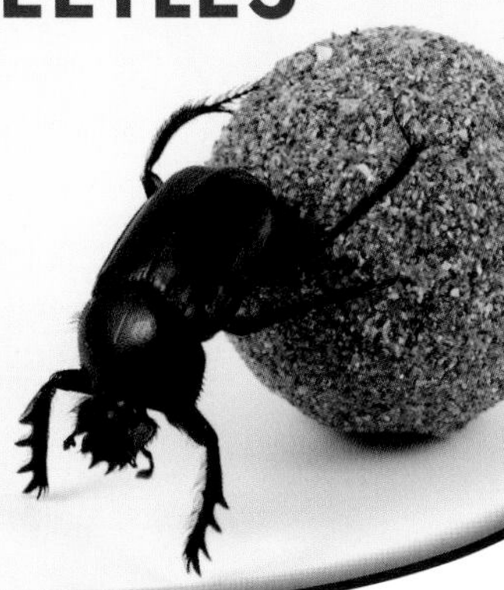

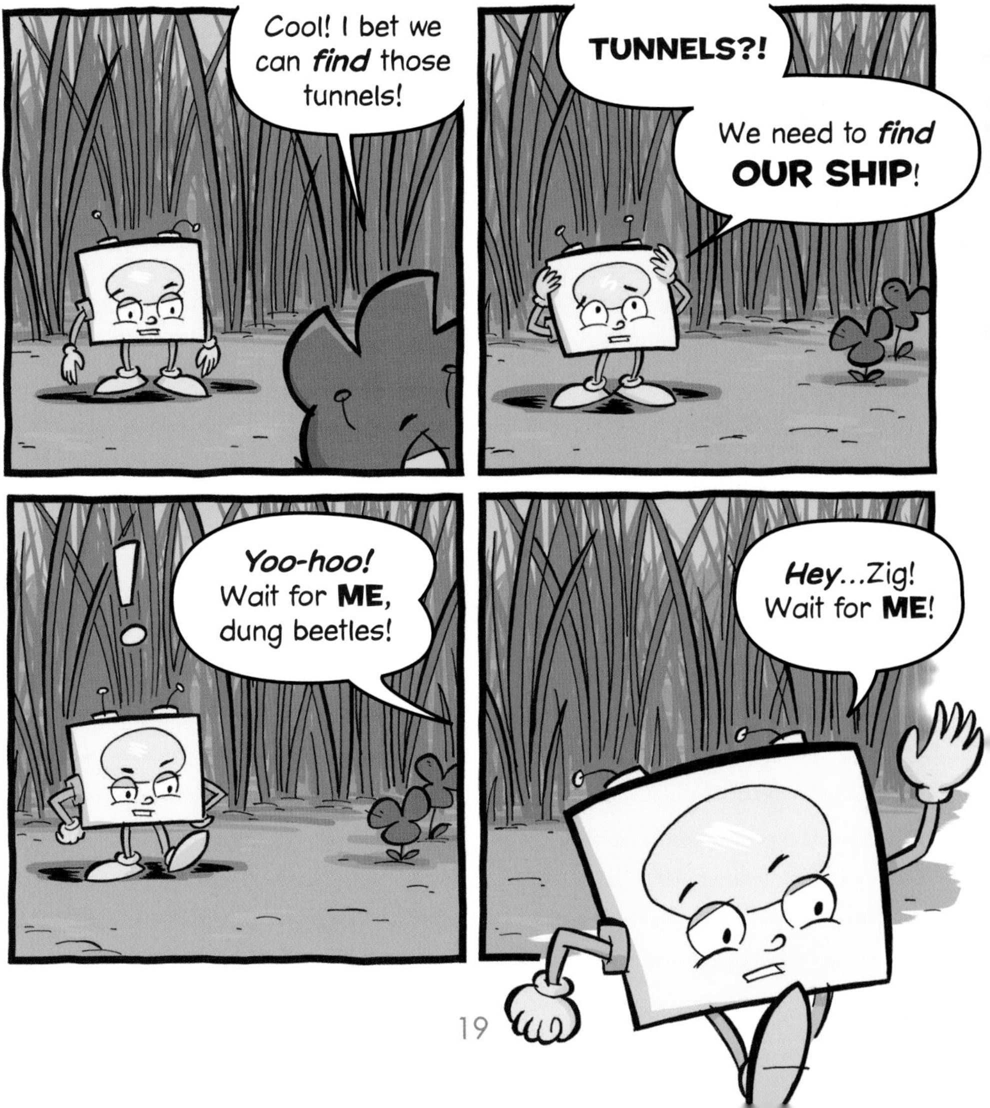

Cool! I bet we can *find* those tunnels!
TUNNELS?!
We need to *find* **OUR SHIP**!
!
Yoo-hoo! Wait for **ME**, dung beetles!
Hey...Zig! Wait for **ME**!

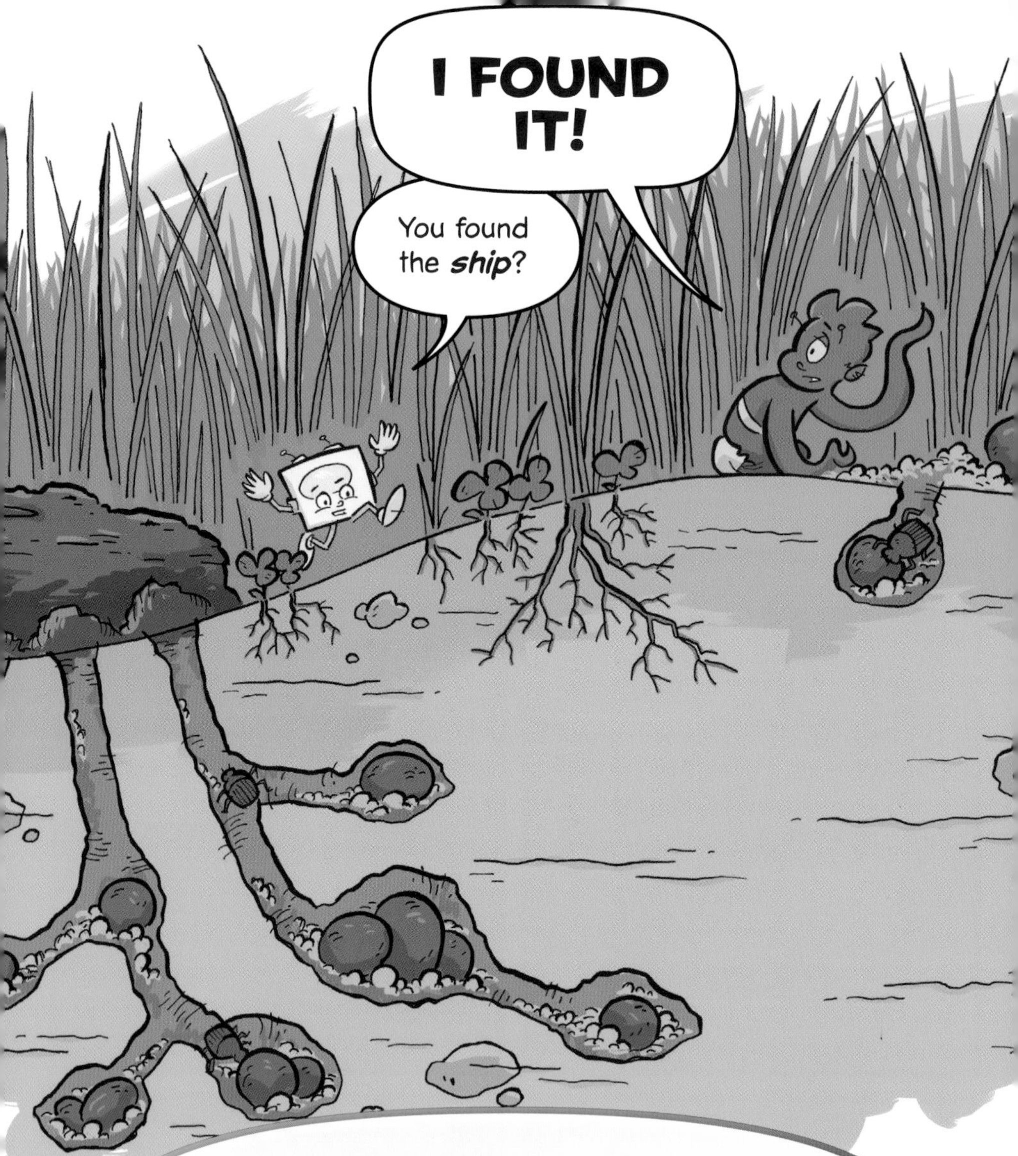
I FOUND IT!
You found the *ship*?

DECOMPOSERS

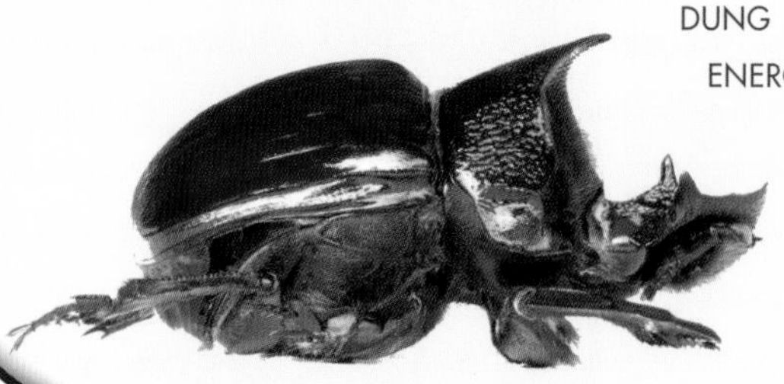

DUNG BEETLES MAKE USE OF THE ENERGY IN THE GRASS LEFT IN A COW'S DUNG. THEY ALSO LAY THEIR EGGS INSIDE IT.

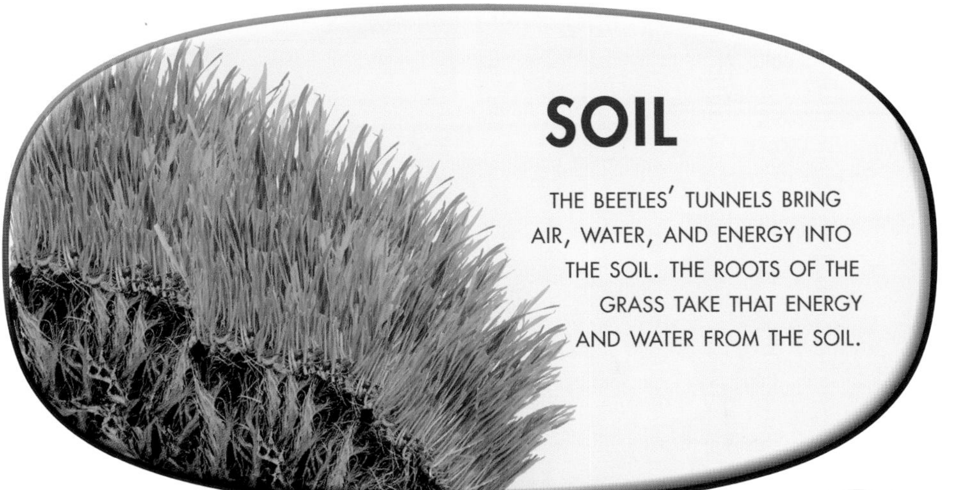

SOIL

THE BEETLES' TUNNELS BRING AIR, WATER, AND ENERGY INTO THE SOIL. THE ROOTS OF THE GRASS TAKE THAT ENERGY AND WATER FROM THE SOIL.

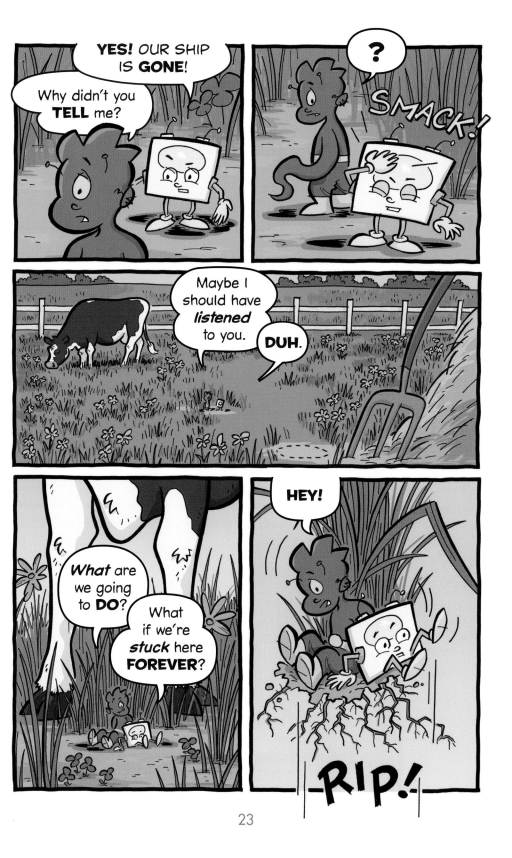

23

28

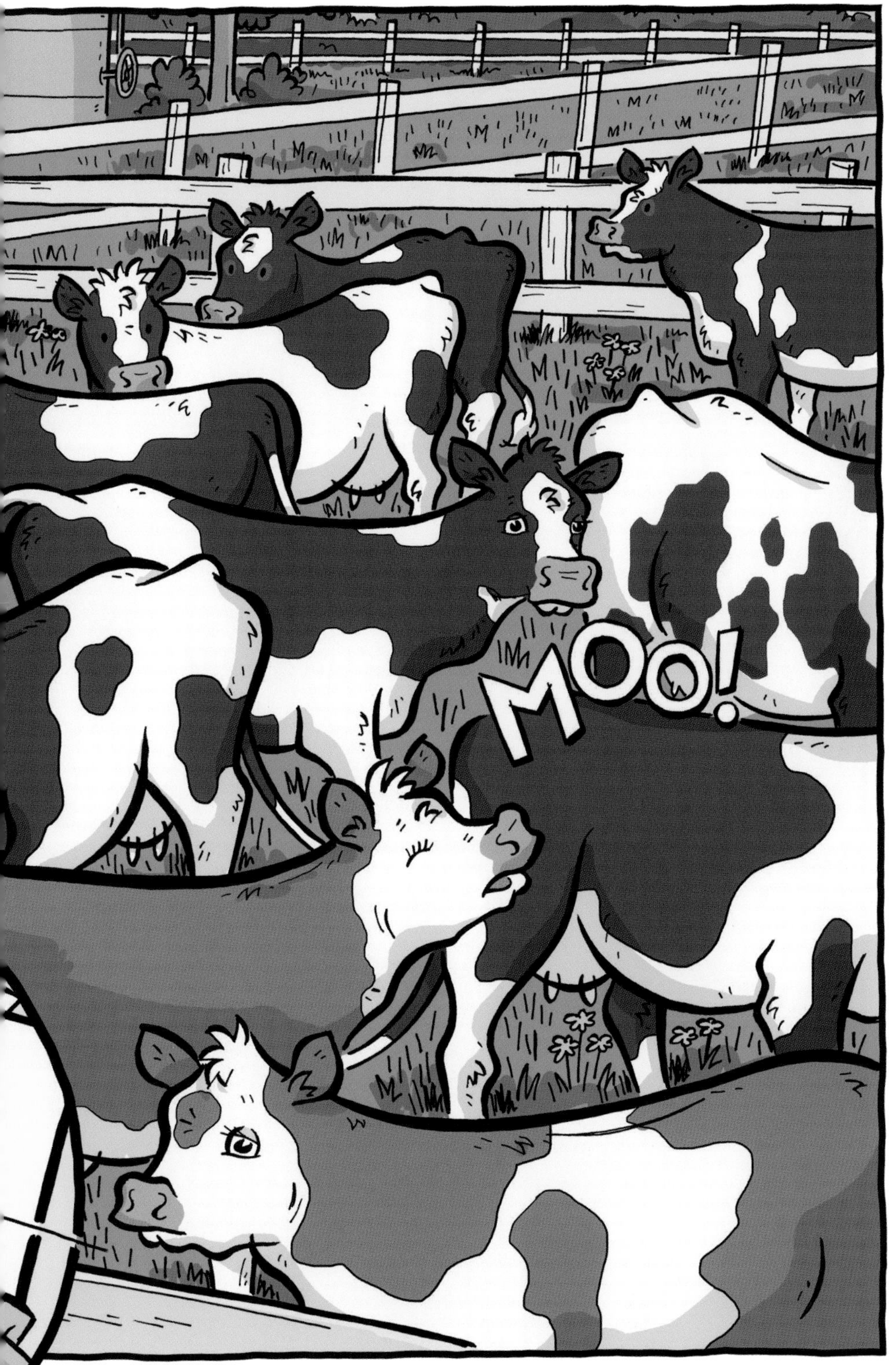
MOO!

32

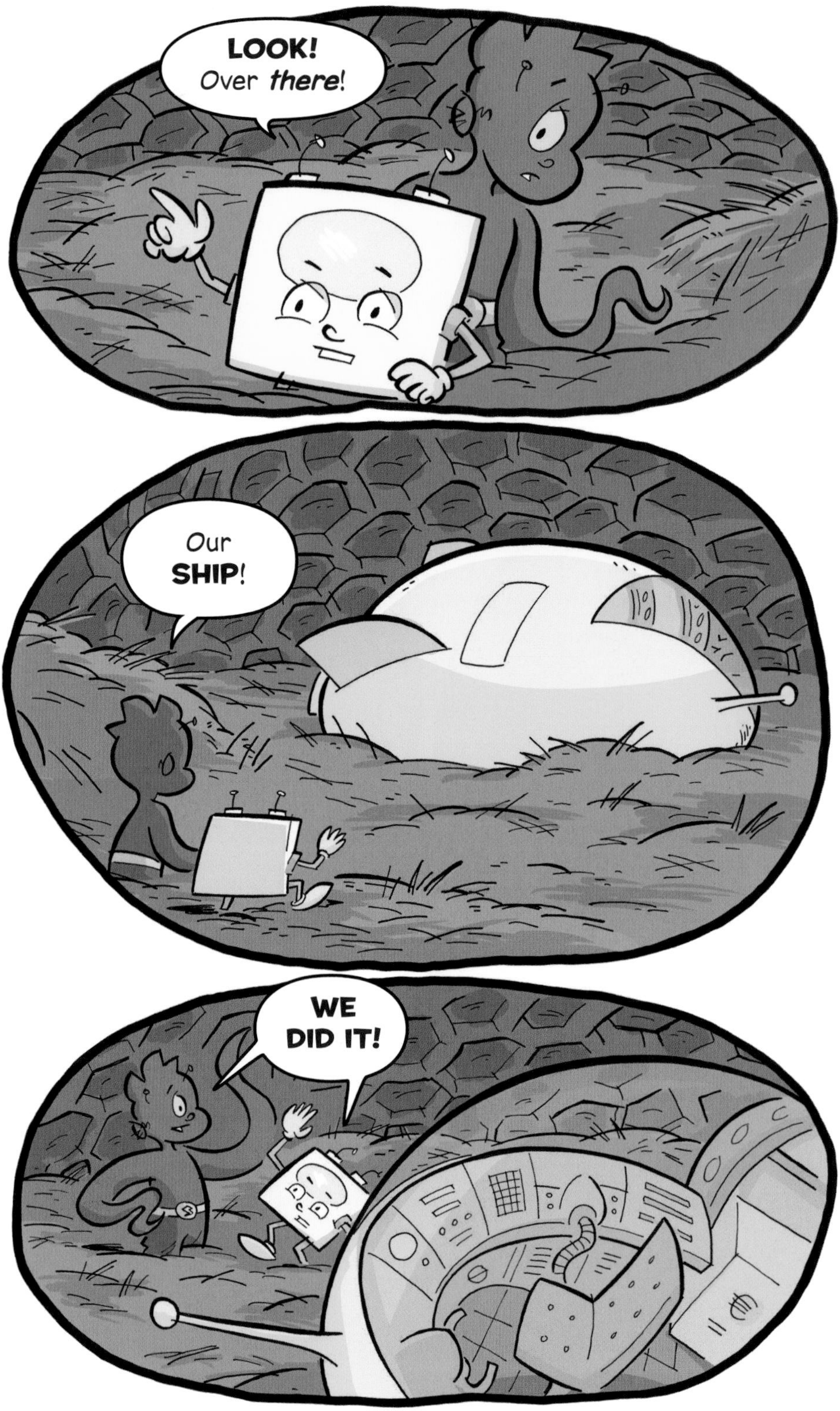

LOOK! Over *there*!
Our **SHIP**!
WE DID IT!

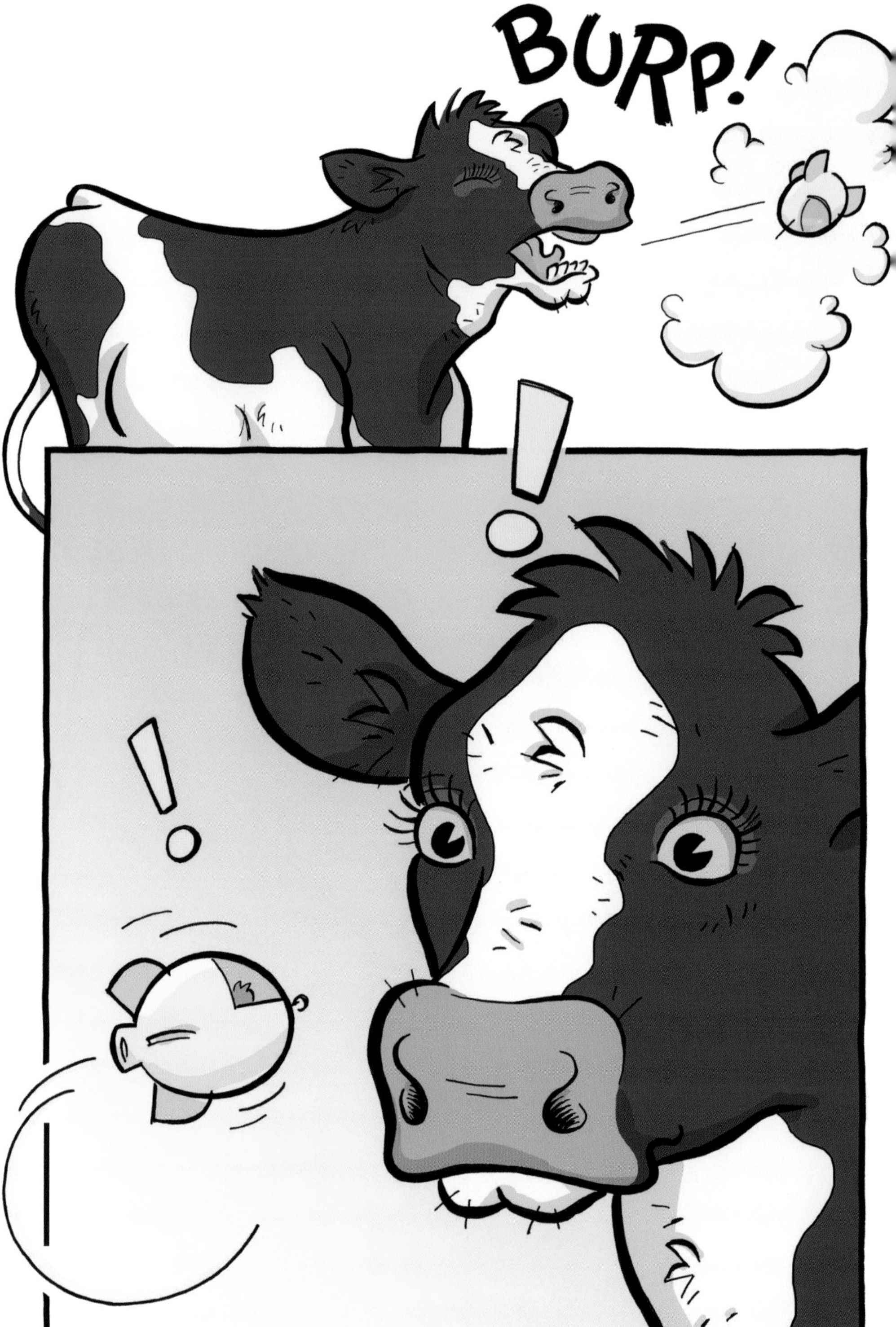
BURP!
!
!

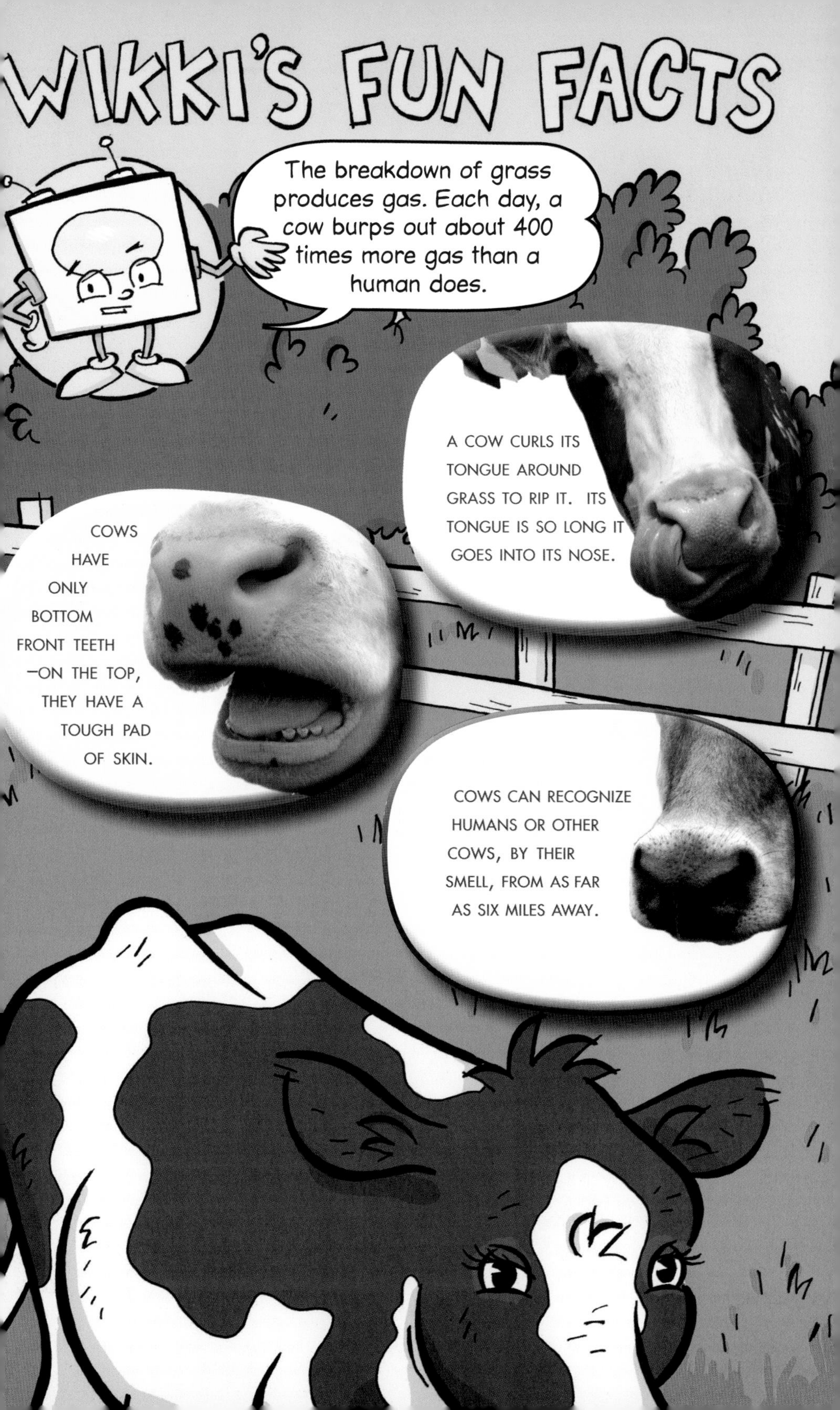
WIKKI'S FUN FACTS
The breakdown of grass produces gas. Each day, a cow burps out about 400 times more gas than a human does.
A COW CURLS ITS TONGUE AROUND GRASS TO RIP IT. ITS TONGUE IS SO LONG IT GOES INTO ITS NOSE.
COWS HAVE ONLY BOTTOM FRONT TEETH —ON THE TOP, THEY HAVE A TOUGH PAD OF SKIN.
COWS CAN RECOGNIZE HUMANS OR OTHER COWS, BY THEIR SMELL, FROM AS FAR AS SIX MILES AWAY.

ABOUT THE AUTHORS

NADJA SPIEGELMAN, who writes Zig and Wikki's adventures, likes cooking, writing, and decorating her apartment with furniture found on the street. She grew up in New York City, but loves going on vacation to the countryside. Once, when she was very young, a cow mistook her bright yellow dress for a flower and tried to eat her. She's still a little afraid of cows, but she'd like to learn how to milk one.

TRADE LOEFFLER, who draws Zig and Wikki, lives in Brooklyn, New York, with his wife, son, and their dog, Boo. Trade grew up in Livermore, California, the home of "the World's Fastest Rodeo," an event complete with bull riding and wild cow milking. Although he grew up in a "cow town," Trade has never considered himself a cowboy—even though he does own two pairs of cowboy boots.